# THE
# BAD BOYS

Other Apple Paperbacks
you will enjoy:

*Camp Murphy*
Colleen O'Shaughnessy McKenna

*The Dragon That Ate Summer*
Brenda Seabrooke

*Kidnapping Kevin Kowalski*
Mary Jane Auch

*Into the Dark*
Nicholas Wilde

# THE
# BAD BOYS

*Original title: The Bad Guys*

## ALLAN BAILLIE
*Illustrations by David Cox*

AN
**APPLE**
PAPERBACK

SCHOLASTIC INC.
New York Toronto London Auckland Sydney

ISBN 0-590-48258-0

Text copyright © 1993 by Allan Baillie. Illustrations copyright © 1993 by David Cox. All rights reserved. Published by Scholastic Inc., 555 Broadway, New York, NY 10012, by arrangement with Omnibus Books. APPLE PAPERBACKS is a registered trademark of Scholastic Inc.

12 11 10 9 8 7 6 5 4 3                                    5 6 7 8 9/9

Printed in the U.S.A.                                     40

First Scholastic printing, June 1994

# Contents

*I would like to dedicate* The Bad Guys *to . . .*
*but I'd better not.*

—A.B.

# 1.
# The Crew

If you don't know what's going on, it's a very nice scene.

There's these four little kids and a puppy sitting on a stone wall, with bags of camping things at their feet. They are looking at a broad lake with a few ducks and a tall hill wearing gum trees like a hat. A creek bounces down the hill into the lake and there's a couple of tents and a girl picking flowers. A sagging sign says this is Mulleygrub Camping Ground. And one of the kids is waving at an old car driving away from them.

Lovely, isn't it?

Except the four little kids is us. The Crew.

The kid keeps on waving at Big Brother's car.

"Sweet Eddie . . ." I warn.

He calls out: "Good-bye."

Which is too much, so I push him off the wall.

I mean, we're here in the wilds because Big Brother took out a contract on us from the Heavies — all right, the parents — to dump us. We live in a city hole that is so tough the mice go around with clubs. The Heavies' excuse is that a week away at a camp will be good for us, but we know they are hoping the man-eating sheep will get us.

Sweet Eddie peers up at me from the bottom of the wall. "What was that for, Wheels?" he says.

"Wheels" is me. Short for Big Wheel. I get the ideas and make things happen. I'm the boss, the kingpin, the Captain of the Crew, and nobody ever forgets this — except for Nose, maybe. I don't worry much about the "Big," because I'm not.

"You waved," I say to Sweet Eddie and curl my lip.

"Oh, sorry," Sweet Eddie says, fiddling with his glasses. His old gray coat is flopped all over him and with his yellow hair he looks like a collapsed scarecrow.

I allow him to climb back on the wall.

Sweet Eddie is an embarrassment to us. He is the sort of kid that rescues butterflies. Once we caught him actually *giving back* marbles he'd won from a sniveling kid. He wears the "Sweet" on his name as punishment until he starts to behave properly. He has his moments, but he is our weakest link.

"What do we do now, Wheels?" says Hulk. Hulk is the missing link.

"Shut up, I'm thinking."

"Err . . ." Hulk grunts, and I watch him carefully.

If Sweet Eddie rescues butterflies, Hulk chases crocodiles. He lumbers about like a great black bear,

2

always looking as if he is about to understand something but never quite getting there. His long black hair is held back by a band like a girl's. It looks stupid, but nobody ever tells him that. I've seen him knock down a brick wall with his head.

"Yer always thinking," says Nose, and yawns.

"I got to," says I. "I'm the only one who *can*."

"Oh yeah? Then maybe we oughta go down there and ask where we can put the tent," says Nose.

Nose hasn't got a spectacular hooter, but it's the way he turns it on over a steaming pot that gets him the name. It would be fine if he kept his hooter in the pot, but he doesn't. Sometimes I think he wants to run the Crew.

So I got to stamp on him. "Ask?" I say. "*Ask?* We are the Crew. We never, ever ask!"

"I just thought — "

"I keep on telling you. I'm the only one that does that."

Nose kicks the wall with the heel of his boot but he shuts up.

And Spectre, my white puppy with black patches around his eyes, scampers across the top of the wall and tries to lick my face.

"No! Licking is *nice!*" I shudder and spin Spectre to face the lake and the hill and the girl picking flowers.

"We're not nice, are we, Crew?"

"No!" shout Hulk and Nose.

"No!" shouts Sweet Eddie, a bit late.

3

"In fact we are very, very nasty! We are what, Crew?"

"Very, very nasty!"

"So in this campsite we are going to do — what?"

"Ah . . ." says Sweet Eddie, vaguely.

But Spectre wakes up and says "Rrrr!" and wags his tail at the girl picking flowers.

"Oh yes," says Sweet Eddie. "Terror!"

"Rampage!" says Nose.

"Battle!" says Hulk.

And I smile. "It is a good place for a little evilry."

For we are the Bad Boys.

# 2.
# Terror!

When we go to the movies we cheer Lex Luthor against Superman, back the Joker against Batman, we get annoyed when Indiana Jones escapes again, and we get deeply depressed when Darth Vader does something *good*.

So we sit on the wall like vultures, looking for trouble. And I am working out some deadly plot . . .

When Spectre bounds into attack.

He rockets off the wall and funnels through the long grass, his short legs *whirring* beneath him.

The girl picking flowers gives a little jump.

Spectre bounces around her.

"Oo," she says. She is short, plump, covered in freckles, and she stares at Spectre with enormous blue eyes.

Spectre sees that she is worried and thrashes the grass with his tail.

"Eh, I'm Wheels. C'mere," I say to the girl, squinting. I worked on the squint before the mirror for weeks, to strike mortal fear in anyone I clobber with it.

But what does she say? "Oo, oo, I'm Mary. Oo, oo, does he bite?"

"No," says Sweet Eddie kindly.

"Yes," I say. "And shut up."

"Um," says Sweet Eddie, crushed.

"Where's the guy who runs the camp?" I say.

Timid Mary is still watching Spectre. "Mr. Howard is not here. That dog looks really savage."

"Where's Howard, then?"

"He's gone. He got sick. That dog, is he going to bite me?"

Suddenly Sweet Eddie's voice sounds as slick as a bucket of worms. "He doesn't bite if he's had breakfast."

Nose frowns and looks at Sweet Eddie strangely. Sweet Eddie wobbles his eyebrows until Nose nods slightly.

Then Nose fakes a shudder. "But if he hasn't . . . Oh boy."

"Remember the burglar, Nose?" says Sweet Eddie.

"The burglar? Oh yeah. Terrible."

*I* don't remember any burglar. Something is going on.

"What happened to the burglar?" says Timid Mary.

"We forgot to give Spectre breakfast, and when we came home . . ."

"What, what, what?"

"Oh, it was horrible, you couldn't look. Did we feed Spectre today, Nose?"

"I don't think so . . ."

"What happened, what happened?" Timid Mary stares at Spectre bouncing around her.

"Oh, Spectre ate him," says Sweet Eddie.

And Spectre licks Timid Mary's hand and Timid Mary throws the flowers into the air and gallops toward the tent on the hill.

Like I say, Sweet Eddie has his moments.

# 3.
# The Tribe

Spectre chases Timid Mary round the tent until someone up there throws a pine cone at him. He comes back to us, making out his feelings are hurt.

Nose and Sweet Eddie are leaning on each other and snorting like pigs in mud, but Hulk frowns at me as if I have been keeping a secret from him.

"What burglar?" he says.

Now if Sweet Eddie — even Nose — had asked me that, I would have laughed out loud and said that it was a joke and only a dummy would have missed it. But you don't do that with Hulk.

"I wasn't there," I say to Hulk. "But did you hear what the girl said?"

They're all giving me the dumb look.

"The man that runs this joint is not here. And that means?"

"We can't camp?" Hulk says.

"No."

"He can't tell us where we *can't* put up the tent," says Nose.

8

"Yeah," I mutter. Smart aleck kids I don't need.

"Because he's not here."

"Yeah, ain't that a pity?"

Hulk smiles like he has finally worked it out.

"For a start, where is the best spot in this dump for our tent?" I ask.

Nose and Hulk and Sweet Eddie look around: at the edge of the lake, which is probably crawling with snakes; at the middle of the camping ground, where you die of boredom; and at the spot high on the hill. Now that spot is near the stream, and the gum forest, and it looks over the lake and everything. The sort of place for a pirate fortress. . . . The sort of place for us.

"Up there." Nose points.

"Yes."

"But there's already a tent up there," Sweet Eddie says.

"That's too bad."

"Ah."

"For them," I say.

We pick up the tent and the duffel bags and sling them over our shoulders. We look at each other and sneer. We hiss through our teeth.

"Yeah?" I say and squint.

"Yeah!" they say and curl their lips.

We tramp up the hill toward the pink-and-blue tent, clanging our frying pans and pots, rattling our tent poles, stomping our boots in the mud, rolling our shoulders, and snapping our fingers. Spectre sniffs through the grass, a man-eating tiger on the hunt.

Oh, the Crew on the prowl is a terrible sight, hide your gold, bolt your door, and flee!

The girls in the pink-and-blue tent — the Tribe — must be shaking.

We get to the tent and see Timid Mary pointing her trembling finger at us and talking to the corner of the tent.

I stop in front of Timid Mary, swing my duffel bag to the ground, and look around. From here you are the king of the camp and all the tents, and the lake. If there's any trouble at all you can charge through everything with terrible shrieks. Nothing can stop you. It's *your* lake, and you can fill it with crocodiles . . .

"What do you want?" says Timid Mary, staring at Spectre.

"We might stay up here . . ." I say.

Another girl comes around the tent, grunting. She's wearing a thick anorak and she's carrying some sticks and a tomahawk. You can't see her eyes or anything because she's got wild brown hair tumbling all over her face.

She stops. "Yes?"

Hulk shuffles backwards.

"Alice, these boys have just arrived," Timid Mary says.

Wild Alice looks at all of us through her hair. "Yes, you want something?" She throws the sticks to Timid Mary.

"We're gonna put our tent up here," I tell her.

"You can't come here. Anywhere here," says Wild Alice, waving her tomahawk around.

"Who says?"

"I says. Wanna make something of it?" She tosses her hair back and a mean green eye is glaring at me.

"Yeah," says Sweet Eddie, then he looks across at me. "Yeah?"

Hulk's eyeballs are shunting from Timid Mary to Wild Alice.

Oh yes. I had forgotten one thing about Hulk. Big, mean Hulk can face five dragons and his dad on a bad day, but he seems to have this strange fear . . .

Wild Alice says, "Yeah," and looks Hulk in the eye.

Hulk hides behind Sweet Eddie.

11

"Nobody lives up here but us." Wild Alice bends over and hits a tent peg with the blunt end of the tomahawk, and the peg rings like a busted bell and disappears in the ground.

Timid Mary stops being timid and stands up. "Yes, it's our mountain."

Two other girls come out of that forest with armfuls of branches. The little one, the really little one, buzzes around the other one like a fly. The Fly does not worry me at all, she makes *me* look like a giant.

"And this is Wendy," says Wild Alice.

It's the other one. Wendy. Big Wendy. She is built like a tree and with all the branches in her arms she *looks* like one. Hulk is staring at her, and he is realizing that she is almost as big as him.

He is about ready to bolt.

My gallant Crew is about to stampede from a tribe of girls in a pink-and-blue tent, unless I do something quickly.

I decide on a bit of quick diplomacy. "Well, what

about letting us put our tent way over there? That's not even as high as you."

"No."

Big Wendy and the Fly drop their bundles of branches on the ground with a crash. They move down on us and Hulk makes a strangled sound and starts to drag Sweet Eddie away.

"The man in charge, Mr. Howard, he would probably let us camp over there," I say. It always helps to appeal to a higher authority, especially if the higher authority is not around to argue.

"He's gone," Wild Alice says smugly.

"Gone where?"

Wild Alice gives me a sneaky look. "Who knows?"

"He was terribly sick," says Timid Mary.

"Something he ate."

"Might be in hospital."

"If he's lucky."

"Yes, well . . ." I say. "See you around."

And we start to walk down the hill. Just casually.

Timid Mary calls after us: "Oh, love that cute puppy!"

And she looks hungry.

# 4.
# The Nerds

Down the hill is a green-and-silver tent with its roof and its sides looking like they have been ironed. There's some thick-looking kids lying around doing camping things like building a fireplace, or tying together sticks for a dish-rack or a basin stand. A bunch of nerds.

After Wild Alice I want to dodge them, but Hulk is lurching straight for the tent.

A long-nosed kid looks up from his dish-rack. "Oh, hi, I'm Frederick. You're new here, aren't you?"

I give him the squint. "What's it to you?"

He doesn't notice the menace in my voice, he doesn't even see the squint. "You'll like it here. Anything you need, just ask," says Fred. Not just a nerd, but a super nerd.

"We don't need nothing." Hulk is recovering.

"Want breakfast?" says Superfred.

A twitchy kid steps back from his little fire and wobbles toward him with a pot of something black and bubbling.

But Hulk says, "Errrgh," and thumps past the tent. I don't blame him. In the twitchy kid's black mess I think I see a few fried ants.

Fried Ants twitches some more and looks puzzled. He sniffs the black brew and shrugs.

"Ah, you don't want to listen to those girls," says Superfred. "Mr. Howard didn't hardly eat any of our stew . . ."

Fried Ants looks guilty.

Spectre sits in front of Fried Ants and wags his tail. Fried Ants dips a wooden spoon into the pot and offers Spectre some mysterious chunks.

Spectre sniffs once, yelps, and scorches past Fried Ants to the lake. Fried Ants staggers backwards and drops the pot, splattering Superfred and turning the fire into a great ball of ash and smoke.

The Crew marches through the ruins.

"Now that's better," I say.

"They were friendly," says Sweet Eddie.

"Shut up," I say.

We stop on a patch of dry sand, lean on an old tree, and look at the lake before us.

"This is better than the hill," says Sweet Eddie. "Isn't it?"

"Sure it is," I say. "Always better to be close to water."

Nose stomps across the sand to the edge of the lake. He scoops up a handful of water, spits it out and comes back. "It's no good, it's salt."

"There's no snakes in salt water," says Hulk. "I think."

"Yeah, what's wrong with that?" I say.

"You can't drink salt water," says Nose. "Someone's got to get water from the creek. All that way." The creek runs into the lake about ten meters away.

"This is the place for a tent. Let's go," I say.

So we unroll the tent, a green-and-brown army

tent. The green is mold and for sure we are the first guys to put it up since Dad's great-granddad marched with the Romans.

"Ahem."

It is Superfred, visiting with two of the Nerds, a kid with shorts flapping round his skinny legs and a thick kid who's bursting out of his shirt.

The kid with the muscles is grinning at Hulk. This kid has a face sunburnt so pink he looks like he's holding his breath.

Hulk scowls.

Pinky flexes his muscles for Hulk.

"Yeah?" I say.

Pinky peers at our tent with his nose screwed up, and maybe he is *really* holding his breath.

"I don't think you'd better put that tent up there," says Superfred.

"It's not smart," says the weedy Nerd, smiling like a lizard.

I look at them, and they are nowhere as dangerous as the Tribe on the hill. "Who says?" I say.

The Lizard stops smiling.

Sweet Eddie nudges behind Hulk.

"Well . . ." says Superfred.

"Nobody tells us where to go," I say. "Nobody. Right, guys?"

"Yeah," says Hulk and squares his shoulders, just for Pinky.

"Yeah," says Nose and yawns.

"Knuckle sandwich," Sweet Eddie says and shows them one from behind Hulk.

And Spectre actually growls.

Maybe Pinky is impressed by Hulk's shoulders. He smiles weakly and pulls Superfred by the arm. "Come on, Fred, we'd better go," he says.

Lizard lifts his eyebrows. "But . . ."

Pinky shoves Lizard in the side and they scramble away, awed by us.

"Yeah," we grin at each other and rub our knuckles together.

We're the Bad Boys, and don't you forget it.

# 5.
# The Campfire

We have a long battle with the tent. It just wants to sprawl in the sand, but after much hammering of pegs and pulling many ropes and a lot of shouting, it is up. All right, it sags and it looks like a bag of elephants, but it is up.

I put our sinister flag high in the tree. The flag is black like a dead-end lane at midnight, with a laughing skull, and two cobras wrestling. It even frightens *us*. We salute it and survey the territory we have taken over.

There is Wild Alice and her Tribe high on the hill, thinking they are safe, and there is Superfred and his Nerds and their very smart camp, and here is Wheels and his Crew. All that is needed now is a single spark to ignite the evilry . . .

Superfred drops round again. "You really shouldn't — "

"He doesn't hear, does he?" I say. "Pull his ears off."

"All right, all right. I just wanted to invite you

for a campfire we're holding tonight." He is shuffling
backwards, covering his ears.

"Ah." I think about it. "Yeah, we'll be there." If
we wanted we'd be there whether we were asked
or not, so Superfred is using his head.

At sunset the Nerds start a large log fire near
their tent and we drift over. All of us — the Nerds,
the Tribe, and the Crew — are supposed to be great

friends. (Hah!) And for a while it looks that way. We're all singing together, passing the cookies around and drinking our mugs of cocoa. (Of course the Crew call it grog.) Maybe it could even have stayed that way.

Pigs could fly . . .

Anyway, Wild Alice wiggles and sits on a sharp stick and smacks Sweet Eddie for being there. Sweet Eddie is feeding some ants with crumbs and he doesn't know nothing from nothing, so Hulk yells "Oy!" and bops her.

So Superfred does the hero bit, and pushes Hulk in the side and sings out, "You leave her alone!" And the Tribe comes out with "Ooowoo!" So Wild Alice shoves Superfred and says, "How dare you hit him!" and the Nerds say "Oowoowoo!" And Wild Alice says, "*I* get to hit him!" and does.

"You watch it," I say to Wild Alice.

"Yeah?" says Wild Alice.

"Yeah!" say the Crew.

"Yeah?" say the Nerds.

"Oh yeah!" say the Tribe.

"Shut up! Please," says Superfred.

And he almost dies when we do, but the Nice Hour is now over. When the singing gets going again the Crew just has to drown the Tribe and adds a few words to Nerd songs, and when we sway to the singing, the Crew somehow goes left when the others go right.

Then we start telling stories.

Oh, we start innocently enough, telling funny stories — or stories which are supposed to be funny. But when the night grows dark and menacing, the stories somehow become filled with ghosts . . .

Sweet Eddie leans forward so that the flickering fire plays on his teeth and his glasses. He is very good at that. He tells of a huge lumberjack who camped by this lake, possibly in this very place. The bulls were supposed to haul great trees out of the bush and he shouted at them, calling them terrible names and cracking a long whip, but one evening a black storm broke.

The bulls got scared stiff by the lightning and ignored the roaring lumberjack and his slashing whip, and refused to move the log. The lumberjack went purple, bit on his whip, and picked up one of the bulls and hurled it into the middle of the lake.

"The lumberjack glared with his bloodshot eyeballs at the remaining terrified bulls," says Sweet Eddie as thunder rolls behind him.

And Spectre is hunched like a waiting vulture over the glowing ashes.

Sweet Eddie says: "This mad lumberjack took a breath and roared: 'I've had it with you great bags of sausage-meat! I'm gonna throw you all into that there lake!' And the bulls stampeded. Yeah, stampeded, with this hundred-ton log bouncing along behind. But the lumberjack got caught in the bull chains.

"The lumberjack bellowed so loud a few guys

across the ocean got chucked into a volcano to keep it quiet, but the bulls thundered into the lake, until there was nothing left. No bulls, no lumberjack, no cracking whip, not even the hundred-ton log."

Wild Alice and a few of the Tribe begin to sigh shakily.

"But that's not the end," says Sweet Eddie, with lightning catching his razzled hair.

"Oh, no. On dark nights, on stormy, dark nights like this, the mad lumberjack comes out of the lake cracking his great whip, looking for his missing bulls.

"Trouble is, he can't tell bulls from people . . ."

# 6.
# Rampage!

After that the Nerds and the Tribe crawl off to their tents and we wish them good night. The camp is peaceful, except for the thunder and lightning.

Suddenly there is a faint howl from the bush up the hill, and some heavy crashes among the trees. Timid Mary pokes her head out of the Tribe's tent, blinks, and pulls her head in. Then she shoves her head out again, opens her mouth, and screams.

Out of the trees lumbers a dark giant, taller than the tents, with arms so long they are trailing on the ground. The giant's head seems to be missing. There is a sort of hat but there is nothing but a piece of darkness between the hat and the shoulders.

The giant comes crashing through the long grass toward the Tribe's tent, waving its arms about and growling. The sky behind it is flickering.

Further down the slope, Superfred sticks his head out of the Nerds' tent and looks up at the Tribe's tent, then at the Giant. He seems to be trying to say

something but the words get caught in his throat.

Wild Alice heaves herself out of the Tribe's tent and waves a flashlight about her. She sees the giant lurching toward her and for a while she points the flashlight at it, but she forgets to turn it on.

The giant roars and lurches toward Wild Alice. She squeals and turns the flashlight on.

The giant still looks horrible but it can't see because of the flashlight beam aimed at it, so it walks into the back of the tent.

Timid Mary shoots out of the front of the tent, screaming and with her eyes closed.

Wild Alice shouts: "You lousy — " and then Timid Mary knocks her over and keeps on running.

The giant gets tangled in the guy ropes and pulls the back of the tent down. "Rarrwurf!" it says.

Wild Alice raises her flashlight from the ground, making like the Statue of Liberty, but gets flattened by Big Wendy and the Fly. The Fly is still in her sleeping bag.

The giant is sort of coming apart at the seams as it fights the Tribe's tent, but nobody cares now.

Superfred stands outside his tent and shouts, "Watch it! Watch it!" not to the giant, but to Timid Mary, still running with her eyes closed.

Pinky shuffles out of the tent to see what's going on, but Fried Ants and Lizard are still in the tent.

Timid Mary hits the Nerds' tent broadside, and for a little bit the tent refuses to pay any attention to the great lump on its roof. Then it begins to sag, a peg bends, slurps out of the ground, a guy stretches and twangs. Finally the whole mess, the wailing Timid Mary and the tent, slump to the earth, covering Fried Ants and Lizard.

Then the rain comes. Buckets of it, floods of it, washes over the Nerds' flattened tent, the Tribe's sagging tent, over sleeping bags, sheets, pillows, piles of clothes. Over Pinky, Superfred, the hump of Fried Ants and Lizard, over Timid Mary, Big Wendy and the Fly, and best of all, over sodden Wild Alice.

Spectre wriggles from the giant's neck and scoots over to me in the shelter of the gum forest. The giant breaks into three: Its right leg becomes Hulk in his duffel bag, its left leg is Nose, and its body is Sweet Eddie in his overcoat, waving his arms about in jeans legs. They join me in the forest and we all look down at what we have caused.

"That's terrible," Sweet Eddie says.

"Yes, terrible, heeheehee," says Hulk and leans on Nose, who is collapsing on me, wheezing.

This business of evilry is dangerous. For a long time we can't breathe properly.

When we can control ourselves we walk slowly out of the forest. Past the Tribe, hammering pegs into the mud in the rain, past the Nerds standing around their flat tent and dripping.

And reach our tent, standing quietly in the rain. In triumph, I stride to the open flap . . .

Oh, I know all about lakes. They lay about the place, full of weeds and ducks and buzzing insects, and they never move. But this lake, this useless salty lake, this lake is not a proper, normal lake. Nobody tells us this. Nobody tells us that this miserable lake is open to the sea.

So it has tides.

So it is low tide when we put the tent up on a nice dry sandy stretch under a tree. But after a low tide there has to come a high tide . . .

So I splash home.

I stagger round in the water and try to stop falling. I grab hold of a pole. A couple of pots, a hat, and a sweater float past me.

Hulk shouts and flounders into the water, chasing his inflatable bed before it bobs into that rotten sea.

Then we hear someone titter. We look around.

Pinky, Fried Ants, Timid Mary, Lizard, Big Wendy and the Fly, Superfred, Wild Alice — they're all there.

And they're all grinning at us.

# 7.
# Nose at Work

The next day we're huddling around a smoky fire and the mist is rising from the lake. Sweet Eddie starts to run off at the mouth about the magic of it all so Hulk thumps him without my permission. Nose is quietly snoring, asleep but still sitting up. I don't know how he does it.

Well, our tent is standing, catching the light of the rising sun. It's not the best — it looks like it is falling slowly — but it's not too bad. After all, we *did* pull it down last night, carried it until we stopped making splashing sounds, and put it up again in the dark and the rain.

The tree near us looks like some sort of Christmas tree, with its branches carrying sleeping bags, sweaters, shorts, undershirts, jeans, underpants, the flag, the lot. At least the dripping has stopped.

As the sunlight spreads across the campsite we see that the Nerds are not much better off than we are. Their tent is up again, but it doesn't seem quite as neat as before. They are sitting around a feeble fire, surrounded by hanging clothes and sleeping bags. Fried Ants is cooking what smells like burning spaghetti and black toast. The smell is so bad that Spectre is covering his nose with his paws, and I wonder if Mr. Howard is *ever* going to recover.

But the Nerds aren't watching Fried Ants's smoldering breakfast. They're looking up the hill.

The Tribe's tent is sitting in the morning sun, every corner pulled out and the flaps zipped up. There is no sign of anyone. They are all in their dry, warm sleeping bags.

"We should have pushed their tent over properly," says Hulk.

"We still can," I say.

Hulk looks at me in sudden fright.

"Ah, later," I say.

Nose opens an eye and says: "Breakfast."

He throws some more wood on the coals and places a pot on the rising fire. He tips some beans into the pot and leans forward. He turns that nose on.

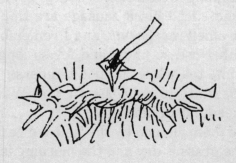

The nose sniffs, wriggles, twitches, and tomatoes join the beans. It snorts, and he throws garlic into the softly bubbling mixture. It breathes very slowly, and herbs and sliced black sausage are tipped into the pot. The smell reaches me and I remember why I put up with Nose so much and for so long. Nose brews up some tea while the pot simmers.

The Nerds start to sniff the air and Wild Alice sticks her head out of her tent.

We ignore them all, and by the time we've finished breakfast the grass is dry and the morning is warm. The Christmas tree is steaming, making its own fog.

"We will have our revenge," I say.

But Nose has gone back to sleep and after a while we all sprawl around him.

I wake up when Lizard runs over me with a bus.

# 8.
# Lizard Attack

Well, I think it's a bus. *Wham*, across my belly. Lizard's shouting from somewhere above me, "Wowowsorrywowahhh!" and he's gone.

I look at my belly and there are muddy bus tracks across my T-shirt. I yell out, "I am killed! Avenge me, Hulk!"

Then I sit up and look around. Lizard has run over me with a bus tire all right, but that's all it is. No wheel in the tire, no hulking machine on the wheel. Just a tire bouncing off the grass, across the sand and into the water. The tire stops and slowly falls sideways and Lizard steps from it. He staggers round in circles until he falls into the water. He pulls himself to his feet and even that he does in circles. He stops, sees me, and falls again.

Spectre finally wakes up and shoots off to punish Lizard for the treacherous attack on his master. He flies over the grass, over the water (no, I don't know how he does it, either), and takes a mighty bound onto Lizard.

To lick him. Sometimes I feel like giving up.

But it's only Lizard, little, weak Lizard. I walk down to the kid in the water. I show him a bunch of five.

"I didn't mean it! They pushed me the wrong way. It was an accident!"

"Yeah, yeah, I've heard it all before." A bop for a start?

"I didn't mean to frighten you, really, Sir."

I stop. "Frighten me? Frighten *me*! Nothing frightens me, ever!"

"Sorry, Captain Sir."

"Frederick was behind it, wasn't he?"

"Yes, they are up on the hill. They made me do it."

I think a thought. "This time you get to live. But I keep the tire you attacked me with, just for a little while. Okay?"

"Okay, okay." And he's off, weaving along the sand with Spectre yapping at his ankles.

I get the tire up and roll it out of the water. The Crew are leaning on each other and watching me, doing nothing.

"What're you doing?" says Nose.

"What *we* are doing is a bit of evilry."

"Yeah? Why?"

"Teach them to grin at us last night."

"Oh, yeah."

"And because they tried to assassinate your Captain."

39

"Ah?"

"Me! Come on, help me with this."

We push the tire past our camp.

"Where are we going?" says Hulk.

"Up the hill," says I.

Nose groans like he's become his Old Man. But we push on.

We pass Big Wendy and the Fly, carrying a few planks.

"What's up?" pants Sweet Eddie.

"We're building a fortress," says the Fly, quickly. "To keep any stupid lumberjack ghosts from bothering us."

"And if any stupid lumberjack ghosts come our way, then they'll be *real* ghosts. Right?" says Big Wendy.

"Right," says Sweet Eddie and ducks his head.

"A fortress won't save them," I mutter as we keep pushing.

"You should have made Lizard push this instead of us," says Nose.

"Shut up," says I.

We stop a little later when Superfred and the Nerds come tramping down the hill.

"You've got our tire," says Fried Ants.

"You hit me with it."

"It was an accident," says Superfred.

"But it was a *good* accident," says Pinky, rubbing his hands together.

"No, it wasn't," says Superfred. "Someone might have got hurt."

"Yeah," says I. "Anyway, we got the tire and we are going to keep it. Okay?"

I straighten my shoulders, Hulk hunches and pulls down his eyebrow, Nose sneers, Sweet Eddie puts his glasses away, and Spectre looks up from a grasshopper. This is going to be a terrible battle.

But Superfred just shrugs and says, "Okay, there's lots more," and the Nerds walk on past.

We watch them go and we get on with the pushing. Finally we reach the forest, and we can see Big Wendy and the Fly putting their planks on the fortress they are building.

"Maybe they are making it too strong," Nose says and he stops pushing the tire.

"Who says we are after the Tribe?" I say. I lean the tire against a tree while I survey the landscape for a useful target.

We see Lizard floating on a round drum in the lake.

"Where are they getting all this stuff?" says Sweet Eddie, putting his glasses back on.

"Ah . . ." I say. Maybe we should have asked around a bit.

And then I see Wild Alice and Timid Mary carry a flagpole from a gully down the hill.

"There!" I shout. "There be treasure! Charge!"

And we do, abandoning the tire for greater booty.

# 9.
# Ship!

Oh, it is a glorious charge. But it's not perfect. Spectre veers off to yap at Big Wendy and the Fly in their fortress until the Fly bounces from the fortress, yaps back, and tries to nip him on the nose. Meanwhile we are shouting, yowling across the hill, causing little avalanches with our stamping feet.

Timid Mary squeals and runs off with her end of the flagpole, pulling Wild Alice behind her. Superfred runs to put himself between them and our thundering charge, but Pinky and Fried Ants are running off in another direction. Superfred grabs the flagpole and runs off with Wild Alice and Timid Mary.

Then we stop. The gully and everything in it is ours.

There are thick poles, thin poles, planks, and pieces of rope. There are round drums, square tins, and string. There are sticks, slats, rusty pieces of machinery, old tires. Piled under trees, thrown onto grass, hanging from branches.

Treasure.

"But what do we do with it?" says Hulk.

I walk around and pick up an empty kerosene tin. "We are the Crew. We build a ship."

"A *ship*?" says Nose.

"Oh, a raft," says Sweet Eddie.

"A *ship*!" says I.

"Okay, okay."

We pick up eight kerosene tins and march to our tent. While we are gone from the gully, Wild Alice and the Tribe race in and take a few more planks, but we don't care. I leave Sweet Eddie to guard the tins and come back for some skinny poles, planks,

rope, and string. After that Wild Alice and Superfred can have the gully to themselves.

We line up four of the tins and tie them to two
skinny poles.

Lizard drifts his round drum toward us, watching,
but doesn't get too close.

We do the same thing with the other four tins.
We use rope to tie poles from one set of tins to the
other, like a square. We carry the creaking mass to
the lake and drop it into the water. Sweet Eddie,
Nose, and Hulk, they all cheer, but I don't. It was
my idea, I *knew* it would float.

Superfred and the Nerds stop rolling tires around
and watch.

We tie planks across the square and sit on it.

"It *still* floats!" says Sweet Eddie in surprise.

I bop him.

Superfred and the Nerds have gone away, even
Lizard.

"Maybe we oughta name it," says Nose.

"Better than that," says I. I go back to the gully,
by myself, for a pole as skinny as a broomstick.

And I almost get ambushed. Superfred and the
Nerds are there, and Wild Alice and her Tribe are
there, and for a moment I think I am about to be
massacred. But the Tribe are only interested in
planks and the Nerds are just rolling drums around.
I grab my broomstick and bolt back to my ship.

I find a knothole in one of the planks and shove
the broomstick in it.

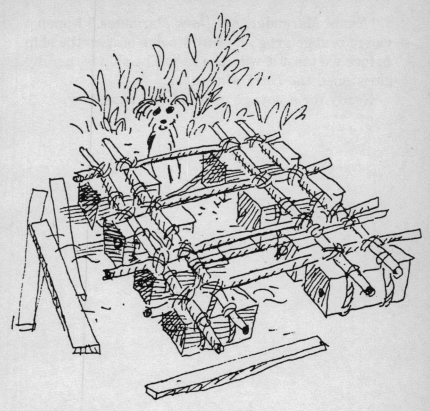

"Oh, a mast," says Nose, and ties string from the top of the broomstick to two corners of the ship.

Hulk brings the black flag down from the tree and ties it on the mast, where it droops.

"That's better," I says. "This is now a ship. What do we call her?"

"I dunno," Hulk says.

"Flying Flounder," Nose says.

"Marauder," Sweet Eddie says.

"Yeah! Marauder, no, *Dark* Marauder." I open a can of orange grog and throw some of it on the ship before we toast it with the rest. The ship is thereby christened the *Dark Marauder*.

Ready for a voyage of blood and treachery.

# 10.
# *Dark Marauder*

Well, we are not so ready for voyages of blood next morning.

After breakfast Sweet Eddie finds a large cog in the gully and ties a rope to it, and we push the *Dark Marauder* out on the lake. We drop the cog in the water and drift.

"What do we do now?" says Hulk.

"Nothing," says Nose and stretches out on the deck.

"Catch fish," says Sweet Eddie, and throws a line out. If there are any fish in the lake they ignore Sweet Eddie. There is nothing on the lake but us and a distant red-and-white buoy with a little flag.

Water slops slowly over the deck, our black flag droops, and nothing happens.

Until Spectre starts barking.

I am lying on the deck looking up at the sky and feeling that the sky is the sea and I am falling up. "Shut up dog, else I throw you overboard."

He doesn't, so I do.

In about three seconds he is back on board, shaking water over everyone. Nose starts muttering about throwing the Captain overboard and Spectre starts barking again.

This time Sweet Eddie turns to see what Spectre is barking at. "There's another raft . . ."

Superfred and the Nerds are sitting on a huge construction of round drums and thick poles. On top is the fly from their tent. One side of the fly is anchored to the deck but the other side is up in the air, tied to the top of two sticks. The Nerds are sitting in the shade of the fly. The ship is tethered to a tree and looks like half a tent on a rubbish heap.

"How d'you like it?" calls Superfred. "It's called the *Golden Eagle*."

"Yes, yes, great," I say.

The Crew get to the shore and huddle.

"We got to do something about *Yellow Chicken*," I say.

"You mean outflash?" says Sweet Eddie.

"You mean do something they haven't?" says Nose.

"Yes, yes. What?"

"No worries."

Nose goes back into the gully. He finds a kerosene tin with its top torn off and hammers it flat. He brings it back to the *Marauder*, puts it on the deck. Sweet Eddie puts rocks on the edges of the flattened tin, Hulk unloads some small pieces of wood, and we push off again.

Superfred calls out, "What are you doing?" He is sitting under the fly of *Yellow Chicken* eating an apple. We ignore him.

Hulk piles some of his small wood on the flattened tin and lights a fire. Nose cooks a bubbling mixture of beans, chili, and cheese in a pot. And we have lunch afloat.

Elegant, I say. Even though we have to keep on saving the fire from the ripples that keep crossing the deck.

Superfred sees what we are doing and has the Nerds pull *Yellow Chicken* ashore.

The lake is ours again. We let the ripples put out the fire and eat on in peace.

Until Superfred takes *Yellow Chicken* to sea again

with some sort of oven of drying clay. It looks like
a small volcano set on the deck.

"He is beginning to annoy me," I say, and send
Sweet Eddie furtively over the side.

We begin to smell smoldering chicken and make
signs that the stink is polluting the atmosphere. The
Nerds make signs that *we* are polluting the atmosphere.

Sweet Eddie returns, dripping but triumphant.

Fried Ants pulls a chicken leg — half burnt and half dripping raw — from the volcano and shakes it at us. The Nerds around him are trying to grin in triumph, but Lizard stares at the chicken leg in horror.

We wave good-bye to them.

For a while they are unable to work out what we mean. But Lizard keeps looking at us and then at the shore. He says something to Superfred, and Superfred grabs the mooring line and pulls it in, showing increasing urgency. But the end of the rope isn't around the tree any more, it's in his hand.

I smile at Superfred.

Superfred yells at the Nerds and they all lie on the deck and paddle with their hands. And then they jump from *Yellow Chicken*, grab it and kick their feet behind it until it is back to shore. Then they lie on the deck, sighing and groaning, with the muddy volcano in the middle of them.

While all this is going on the Tribe are sitting in their fortress, looking on.

# 11.
# Foul Deeds

I am looking at the dead bodies on *Yellow Chicken* and I am thinking.

Sweet Eddie steams up his glasses and says: "What we need is paddles."

"Was thinking of that," I says.

Sweet Eddie and Spectre stay on the *Marauder* to protect it from a sneak attack, while the rest of us creep into the gully. We find some short planks and Nose finds some slats that are more bendy and brings them along, too. Nose won't say why he wants them.

We walk straight into Superfred and the Nerds.

"Watch it," says Hulk.

"Oh yeah?" says Pinky.

"Any time," says Hulk.

"Say the word," says Pinky.

And we go past each other.

We get on the *Marauder* and paddle it from shore with the short planks.

"It's hard work," Nose says.

"We should make the planks look like paddles," says Sweet Eddie.

So we go back and draw the shape of paddles on the planks and use our knives and the hatchet to get the planks just a little bit like the drawings. Sweet Eddie's plank looks more like a duck than a paddle but we're getting there.

We take the *Marauder* out again and it's much better now. We can push it along so fast that it makes a little bow wave, but there's too much water going over the deck and after a while the paddles hurt our hands.

We stop.

"Maybe we could wrap tape around the paddles' handles," says Sweet Eddie.

"Forget it, Sweet Eddie," I say. "We're tough."

"Yeah," says Hulk.

Spectre starts to bark again and *Yellow Chicken* is moving out onto the lake. Superfred and the

Nerds are kneeling on the ship's sides, pushing their paddles into the water with some sort of rhythm.

"One, two, let us go," they are chanting, and *Yellow Chicken* is picking up speed. There is no line to the tree this time and *Yellow Chicken* is aimed at the *Marauder*.

"Paddle, paddle!" I shout, but it is too late.

*Yellow Chicken* creams past the *Marauder* like we are a rock. The Nerds cheer, and as they move away Pinky lobs a banana skin at Nose. It hits him full in the face.

Nose fingers the skin from his face. "Now?" he hisses through his teeth.

"Right," I say. "This is war!"

# 12.
# The Challenge

We paddle the *Marauder* ashore and lift it out of the water. We are not ready for a naval engagement yet.

"It's too low in the water," says Nose.

"Someone eats too much," I say. My design is being abused.

"Put more tins underneath," says Hulk.

I think of thumping Hulk but decide against it. "All right," I say.

We get a few more kerosene tins and return to the *Marauder*. There aren't many tins left now. We undo some of the ropes and lift the planks and the frame from the tins.

"We should change these," says Nose and kicks at one of the rows of tins.

"What's wrong with them?" I ask.

"The tins are square up front. We got to push them through the water. They should be like a boat, with a point up front."

"How are you going to do that?"

About then Pinky wades across from *Yellow Chicken* and leers. "You rebuilding that wreck? Won't do any good, yer gonna get creamed anyhow."

"Who says?" says Hulk.

"Me says."

"Yeah?"

"Yeah!"

About then Wild Alice lobs in. "They're nice rafts, aren't they?"

"One is," says Pinky.

"It's a ship," I say.

Superfred comes ashore. Everyone is tramping through our camp.

"Going to have a race?" says Wild Alice.

"Race?" Pinky and Nose stare at each other.

"Oh yes," says Superfred and claps his hands. "That's a very good idea, don't you think so?" He looks at me.

I look at Nose and Hulk and then at Pinky. I smile. "Yeah, we'll have a race."

"All you girls will have to come down and watch," says Superfred.

"Oh no," says Wild Alice. "We'll be in the race, too."

I look up the hill and the fortress doesn't exist any more. It is being carried down the hill by Timid Mary and Big Wendy and the Fly.

I don't smile, but I remember that there are not too many tins left in the gully. "All right, what's the prize?"

Superfred looks at Wild Alice and Wild Alice looks at Superfred.

Wild Alice looks at Nose and maybe she is remembering the smell that comes from our camp around mealtime.

"Tell you what," she says, going all cunning, "the losers have to cook a dinner for the winner."

Us, the Crew, the Bad Boys, the tough ones, serving a meal to Superfred and his Nerds? Worse, worse, us cooking for Wild Alice and the Tribe!

I begin to shudder. But no, it can't happen, it's impossible. The Bad Boys can't be beat.

I smile sweetly at Wild Alice and Superfred.

"Sure," I say.

# 13.
# The Secret Weapon

The first thing we do is get the Tribe and all the Nerds out of our campsite. Then we organize our tent. We throw out everything in the tent and carry in all the kerosene tins. And we close the flaps and put Hulk on guard duty. We are very serious about this.

"Now, we were going to put a point on these tins . . ."

Nose looks at the two lines of tins on their sides, the way they were under the *Marauder*, like railway tracks. Then he opens his eyes, as if he's been asleep for about five years.

"Easy," he says and he sounds like someone has whacked him on the head with a rubber bat. He bends over, picks up the end of one line of kerosene tins and moves it to the end of the other line, making it look like a big arrowhead. Not quite a point, because the kerosene tins still have square ends, but we're getting there.

And then Sweet Eddie adds one more tin. All the

other kerosene tins are on their sides, but Sweet Eddie makes his tin stand up in the space where the lines of tins meet, giving them a perfect point.

Nose adjusts the ropes to shift the tins just a little. The lines of tins don't look like an arrowhead any more, they look like the outline of a boat. A few other tins are added.

We come out of the tent cautiously but we can see only Big Wendy and the Fly carrying a round drum and two kerosene tins to a distant curve of the shore and no sign of Superfred and the Nerds at all.

We go over to the deck of the *Marauder* with the idea of carrying it into the tent and finishing the ship there. We lift it . . .

"This is heavy!" Sweet Eddie says.

"Shut up, wimp," I pant.

"Hang on," Nose says, and puts his corner down. Sweet Eddie and I put ours down, too, but Hulk is left to think about it. "It'll get heavier when we attach the tins. It's going to be murder!"

Hulk puts down his corner.

Okay, we move the tins — and the tent — into the water. We pitch the tent in knee-deep water, and we figure by now the tent must be getting used to it. We then carry the deck of the *Marauder* into the tent and set it on the tins.

Of course it doesn't fit.

"There's too much wood in the deck," says Nose.

So we undo knots, take away several planks and skinny poles and tie knots again. We push the *Ma-*

*rauder* from end to end of the tent and it now feels light and moves like a fish. We get on and it still glides about. We'd like to take it out of the tent, but we don't want to show the enemy what they are up against. Not yet.

So we close the tent on the *Marauder* and wade ashore. We sit around under the tree and cook our dinner, watching the Tribe running around trying to make their raft float. The Nerds come our way and see our tent in the water again and fall about laughing. They can have their giggles today. It's tomorrow that counts.

When the sun sets we slide the *Marauder* from the tent, sit on the edges, and work our paddles. We sit high now, with the deck not even touching the water. We feel like we are almost flying. The *Marauder* is sliding across the lake like a great black bat.

"This is lovely," says Sweet Eddie and this time he doesn't even get thumped.

And then Nose pulls out his supple slats and shows us what they are for.

"Ah," says I.

"Oh yes," says Sweet Eddie.

"Heeheehee," says Hulk.

Now the *Marauder* is not only the fastest ship on the sea, but it is also a battleship.

We get back to the tent and Sweet Eddie unscrews the cap on the tin that stands at the bow, the only cap above water.

"What d'you want to do that for?" I say. "You want to sink us?"

Sweet Eddie picks up the broomstick with the black flag and puts it in the hole. Then he lights a candle and drips the wax around the hole until the hole is sealed and the broomstick is held rigid.

"Why are you doing that?" Hulk says.

" 'Cause I've taken the cap off and I can't put it back. I've got to keep the water out, haven't I?"

"Else we'll sink," I say.

Hulk drops his hairy brow over his eyes and stays like that while we lay our sleeping bags under the tree. Then he goes out into the night.

After a long time he comes back with a clinking handful.

"What've you done?" I shout. "You've taken the caps from our tins!"

"No," he says. "Theirs."

# 14.
# The Race

Next morning we get woken by the stench of soggy porridge and charred damper. Fried Ants is cooking up a victory breakfast for the Nerds. We think the Nerds may not survive for the start.

But they are tougher than that and they push *Yellow Chicken* into our cove. Pinky and Lizard keep grinning at us, as if they are looking forward to us cooking their dinner.

They can dream. We grin back.

Especially after we have a sly look at *Yellow Chicken*. They don't seem to have changed anything about their ship, but Hulk has.

We were worried that Hulk had sunk *Yellow Chicken* overnight, and Superfred would have been able to fix it in time for the race. But Hulk has suddenly become a genius. I don't know where he got that from.

You see, the cap holes are high on the round faces of the oil drums, so with everyone pushing *Yellow Chicken* and nobody sitting, no water has got inside the drums. But this will change when Superfred and the Nerds leap on top and start to paddle.

"Heehee," says Sweet Eddie.

I bop him myself.

The Tribe paddle their raft alongside *Yellow Chicken*, and even Superfred has trouble keeping his face straight. This one is low, so low it is almost a submarine. There is a round drum up front, two kerosene tins on the sides, and two air beds in the middle. There is a mast, a flagpole with some sort of pink bandage on one side of it. The Tribe's raft looks like a skewered sandwich.

"That's nice," says Superfred.

"Thank you very much," says Wild Alice sweetly.

"What do you call it?" says Superfred. "Ours is the *Golden Eagle*."

"Oh, that is very nice. Ours is the *Flamingo*."

"Flamingo?"

"Pink bird. It looks clumsy standing in the water, but when it flies . . ." She smiles at Superfred and me.

"Oh, those pink wings," says Big Wendy.

"Wow," the Fly says.

"Well, where do we race to?" Like I am not listening.

Wild Alice sticks her finger in her mouth and holds it up to the breeze. "Why not race out to that thing out there?" She points at the red-and-white buoy with a flag.

"And back," says Superfred.

"And back?" She seems worried.

"We have to come back," says Superfred.

Wild Alice shrugs. "Okay, let's go."

Nose, Hulk, and Sweet Eddie paddle the *Dark Marauder* slowly from the tent into the morning sun. The black flag lifts in the breeze and Spectre growls fiercely from the box in the middle of the ship.

"Oo," says Timid Mary.

I climb aboard the *Marauder*, pick up my paddle, and look down at *Flamingo*. Big Wendy growls at me and the Fly growls at Spectre.

"Who says Go?" says Wild Alice.

"I do," says Superfred.

"Fine," I say and the Crew start paddling flat out.

"Hey, I haven't said Go yet," says Superfred, then: "Ah nuts, Go!"

# 15.
# Battle!

With Spectre yapping at us like a road drill we slide out from the shelter of the shore. I look over my shoulder and see *Yellow Chicken* rock as Fried Ants and Lizard fumble for their paddles. It starts to pick up speed but wanders off sideways. *Flamingo* has not moved.

"Shut up, Spectre," I say. "Easy now."

*Marauder* is slicing through the water and we only have to paddle a little bit to keep up the speed. But Superfred and the Nerds are chanting fast now, getting serious with their paddling and everything. They seem to be catching up with us, which is fine by us.

"They still aren't coming!" Sweet Eddie shouts from behind me.

"Who?"

"The girls — the Tribe."

"Oh, them. Don't worry about them. They are still working out which end of a paddle to use."

69

"One, two, three, we serve them lumps for free."
*Yellow Chicken* is getting closer.

"They're fiddling with the mast," Sweet Eddie
yells.

"Who?"

"The Tribe. They're making a cross out of the
mast."

"One, two, four, we make them plenty sore."

"Forget about them. Ready stern cannons." Hulk
and I paddle on as Sweet Eddie and Nose change
*Marauder* into a battleship.

That's the plan.

"Oh," says Sweet Eddie.

I look over my shoulder and see Nose jamming
the end of one of his special supple slats between
two of the planks. That is what he should be doing,
but Sweet Eddie is holding his slat like he can't
remember what to do with it. He is looking back,
and *Yellow Chicken* is almost level with the *Marauder*'s stern. But he's not looking at *Yellow
Chicken*, he's looking back, way back, to *Flamingo*.
I look, too.

"Treachery," I say.

Because they've turned that vertical pink bandage
on the mast so it is horizontal, so it runs straight
across the mast. And they've pulled the pink bandage out and it is a pink sheet. Or was. They have
tied the bottom two corners of the sheet to *Flamingo*'s front corners, so the pink sheet is now a
big sail.

"They can't do that," says Sweet Eddie. "Can they?"

"Never mind them," I say as *Yellow Chicken* surges alongside. "Load cannon!"

"Two, four, eight, stand aside, navigate!"

Nose reaches into the box, Sweet Eddie jams his slat between two deck planks and reaches for a very, very ripe tomato. Nose and Sweet Eddie bend their slats halfway to the deck and place their tomatoes on the slats.

The Nerds suddenly realize what is happening and stop paddling.

Superfred says: "Stop — "

I say: "Fire!"

The slats are released and the red missiles arc across the water. One misses *Yellow Chicken* entirely and splashes into the water on the other side. But the other, well, the other one explodes on Superfred's chin, smearing his white shirt with red, dumping lumps of goo over his mouth and nose. Superfred coughs and shakes his head and spits for a long time.

*Yellow Chicken* stops dead in the water and the *Marauder* glides on its way.

Then — double treachery!

Something hits me on the back of the head and I am suddenly wet. I look about me and the *Marauder* is being bombarded by water bombs. The Nerds are hauling ready-filled balloons from under their deck planks and hurling them at us.

I am shocked. To think that a fair, honorable person like Superfred would plot to attack an innocent competitor in a friendly race. Disgusting!

"Load all cannons," I say, grabbing my slat and a handful of mud from the box.

A paper water bomb hits the deck near where Spectre is yapping at the enemy. Spectre yelps, abandons ship, and swims for shore.

"No bones for you tonight," I say. "Fire at will!"

"Who's W — ?"

"Shut up and fire!"

Pinky hits Sweet Eddie with a flour bomb. "That's for you, bum — "

And he gets hit with a tomato in the ear, a mud missile in the hair.

"Stand firm, men!" says Superfred.

Sweet Eddie, with flour all over his glasses, throws mud at the sound of Superfred's voice, and scores.

Fried Ants and Lizard combine to bomb Hulk, Nose bombs Fried Ants, Superfred aims at me and misses . . .

And *Flamingo* sails past us, looking a bit like a Viking longboat with the Tribe just sitting, not paddling or anything, just sitting and watching us.

"Hey, maybe we better paddle," says Sweet Eddie. He gets hit with a water bomb, turning his flour to paste.

"Shut up and throw."

We give up on the cannon and stand up to pitch everything we can get our hands on. Tomatoes, flour mixed with sour milk, vegetable waste, tea dregs,

mud, even some of the water bombs they'd thrown at us which hadn't burst. But after a while the throwing dies out and we just stand and peer at each other.

They look like walking rubbish heaps, dripping and panting. We are even worse. And in the distance *Flamingo* is going round the buoy. The Tribe is putting the sail away and beginning to paddle.

"Hey!" says Pinky. "We're sinking!"

"Heeheehee," says Hulk.

# 16.
# The Sinking

Once *Yellow Chicken* was a massive cruiser, but now it is so low you can see tiny fish swimming over the corners of the decks. Pinky splashes about and sees Hulk's face. He sort of blinks once. He sprawls on the deck of *Yellow Chicken*, sticks his head in the water, and suddenly sits up.

"They've stolen the caps!"

"What?" Superfred frowns at Pinky.

"The caps! On the drums! To keep the water out . . ."

Slowly it dawns. Superfred looks at me and his face gets redder than Pinky's. "Right!" he yells. "Ram them!"

The Nerds immediately sit and pick up their paddles.

"Two, five, ten, now we're gonna smash them." And *Yellow Chicken* starts to turn toward us.

"Paddles!" I shout.

We dive for the deck and try to get the *Marauder* moving. I get a paddle, but Hulk and Nose pounce on the same one and Sweet Eddie can't find anything at all.

Then *Yellow Chicken* hits the *Marauder*. My corner gets kicked into the air and I tumble into the water.

"Help," I say, when I get a floating lump of tomato and flour out of my mouth.

Superfred looks at me doubtfully. Maybe he is deciding whether to offer me the end of his paddle or hit me with it. Anyway, the *Marauder* twists in the water, and that makes *Yellow Chicken* slide sideways, and that dumps Superfred in the drink.

*Yellow Chicken* runs over him and he disappears.

"Help," I try again. Swimming is something I do not do.

*Flamingo* comes past, the Tribe paddling it like an emperor's barge. Wild Alice splashes me with her paddle and sneers.

Timid Mary says: "Silly people," and they all ignore us.

"Hey," I say in annoyance. I could be drowning.

The Crew push the *Marauder* out from under *Yellow Chicken* and *Yellow Chicken* snags *Flamingo*.

"Get away, get away!" shouts Wild Alice.

Superfred appears again, or a part of him. His legs are waving slowly in the direction of Wild Alice, but the rest of him is underwater.

The Crew cheer and start paddling away.

"Hey!" I shout at the Crew, who seem to be about to abandon their Captain. I am so mad at this that I try to kick some water at them but I stub my toes in mud. I stand and find the water is only waist deep.

"Come back here, that's my ship!" I yell.

Nose looks a bit annoyed, but he turns the *Marauder* toward me.

I take a step, but the mud is about as solid as porridge. My feet are sinking, I am wobbling, and I am about to fall into the water again. I grab Superfred's waving legs and fall anyway.

So Superfred's head pops out of the water and he looks like he's been given the full mud beauty treatment. He spends some time gasping and wheezing and spluttering and wiping mud out of his eyes. He sees me and clutches me. "You've saved me! You've saved me! Oh, thank you!"

"Get out! Get out!" I am beating him away, but

already I see the look of disgust on the faces of the
Crew.

I pull myself aboard the *Marauder* and mutter,
"I didn't, I wouldn't. Would I?" But I know my
reputation is in peril. So I've got to do something
about it.

"Well?" says Nose, showing his teeth.

"To the buoy, fast." I start paddling.

"We'll never catch *Flamingo*," wails Sweet Eddie.
But he paddles.

"Oh, yes, we will . . ." I say.

I look over my shoulder and Superfred is waving
farewell to me before wading over to the mess of
*Yellow Chicken* and *Flamingo*. *Yellow Chicken* has
got one drum on the deck of *Flamingo* and the tent
fly is caught up with *Flamingo*'s pink sail. The Nerds
and the Tribe are pulling and shoving and shouting
at each other.

The things they are saying to each other . . .

We paddle on for half a minute, halfway to the buoy, then I look back again.

"Okay," I say.

"Eh?" pants Nose.

"They're not looking. Turn about."

"Ah," says Nose.

"Oh," says Sweet Eddie.

"Heehee," says Hulk.

*Yellow Chicken* and *Flamingo* separate before we reach them, and Wild Alice gets the Tribe reaching for their paddles, but they haven't a hope.

The *Dark Marauder* slides past the stuffed, plucked *Yellow Chicken*, and glides past the featherless *Flamingo* with its floppy Tribe.

"Silly people," I say to not-so-Timid Mary and stroke for the beach.

# 17.
# The Winners

**B**ut there is a faint windy rumbling and a distant yapping from high on the hill.

And we stop paddling to see what it is.

Spectre is on the chase: fast as a cheetah, fierce as a tiger, he's trying to kill the bus tire we'd left at the edge of the forest. But it's rolling, getting faster with every bounce.

It hurtles toward the Tribe's tent, and the Tribe stop paddling to shudder and gasp.

Spectre nips at the tire and it wobbles past the Tribe's tent. The Tribe sigh.

It thunders toward the Nerds' tent and the shipwrecked Nerds groan pitifully.

It bounces over the Nerds' tent, and Superfred wipes mud from his mouth. It scuds along the side of the gully, scythes through the grass, and blasts toward the lake.

"Um," says Sweet Eddie.

It hits a large rock and soars into the blue sky to hover over us.

"It's going to hit!" shouts Sweet Eddie.

"Don't be — "

We all jump into the water.

The tire plummets to the *Dark Marauder*, breaking the mast, sinking the flag of skull and twin cobras, shuffling the deck planks, and spinning off into the lake. It is a black moment.

And *Flamingo* cruises past us to the shore.

"We won!" shouts Wild Alice and the Tribe. Not-so-Timid Mary, Big Wendy and the Fly dance around on the deck.

Superfred and Pinky and Fried Ants are pushing *Yellow Chicken* tiredly out of the lake. Lizard is slowly gathering the balloon and paper fragments from the area of the Nerds' lost battle.

Nose and Hulk and Sweet Eddie and I are sitting, drooping, in the water and looking up at the Tribe and their ship.

"We've won," crows Wild Alice.

"Yeah . . . you won," I say, looking desperately for a way out.

"You owe us a dinner," says Wild Alice, looking hungrily at Nose. Thinking of the lovely smells that floated from his cooking fire.

But Superfred is shouting, "We'll cook, we'll cook!"

"Hey?" says Wild Alice.

"Anything for our mate," says Superfred. "He saved me, you know."

"Yeah, what he said," says Fried Ants.

Wild Alice stares at Superfred and Fried Ants, and she is remembering the smells that came from Fried Ants's fire, and Mr. Howard, who had eaten there once and is somewhere in the hospital recovering.

"Oh," says Wild Alice.

And I smile at her.

See, the Bad Boys can't be beat.

# About the Author

ALLAN BAILLIE was born in Scotland, but moved to Australia when he was seven years old. After leaving school, he worked as a cadet journalist at the Melbourne *Sun* newspaper while studying for a Diploma of Journalism from Melbourne University.

Allan Baillie is the author of several award-winning books for children, including: *Megan's Star*; *Drac and the Gremlin*; *Adrift*; *Little Brother*; *Bawshou Rescues the Sun*; and *The Boss*.

Mr. Baillie lives in Australia.

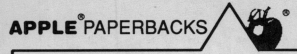